Life

by

Christian McCallister

Copyright 2000, 2021 by Christian McCallister

Any resemblance between any character and any person, living or dead, is purely coincidental, as this is a work of fiction. The same applies to any resemblance between any company in the story and any currently-existing business entity. No part of this publication may be reproduced, distributed, or transmitted in any form or by any means, including photocopying recording, or other electronic or mechanical methods, without prior written permission of the author, except in the case of brief quotations embodied in critical reviews and certain other noncommercial uses permitted by copyright law. Large portions of this novel were dictated using Dragon software.

Prologue

Sage Newton was immortal. He was also quite dead. The other Sages wanted to keep this quiet, but that proved to be impossible. The Sages did an internal investigation to try to figure out how one of their own had died, but there are other ways limitless abilities were blocked by their own enhancements and they began a search for outside help. Where to look? What look? They could not leave the death of one of their own uninvestigated, as the news would eventually get out and the death of an immortal Sage would certainly cause repercussions.

Part One
Before the Trip

Chapter One
The Rites of Spring

On March 1, 2032, the world's largest agricultural company was Harvestman Agricultural Combine. That name had not been around very long, as the entity then known as HAC was the result of acquisitions and mergers spread across several decades. There were pieces of HAC that were two centuries old, and there were holding companies that had been organized, incorporated, and disbanded in two weeks. The entity known as HAC covered every aspect of agriculture known to humankind, including straight farming, colleges of agriculture and animal husbandry, and genetic engineering. Like a mansion spread across acres, there were many nooks and crannies within HAC to hide such things as financial assets and human assets.

A glance through the business section

of the Virtual News Net (VNN) on March 1, 2032 would have led to the conclusion that HAC was part of a trend and it had counterparts in other fields. A good example was the Sutton Group. The Sutton Group had no interest whatsoever in agriculture, except where the interests of agriculture required electronics. The Sutton Group was a mega-corporation that had subsumed electronics companies of every ilk, for decades, and built its own sprawling mansion replete with cubbyholes.

One more counterpart to HAC and the Sutton Group was GenMedico, formerly called General Medical Corporation. It had nothing in common with either HAC or the Sutton Group. It covered every imaginable aspect of the medical field, from hospitals, to medical schools, to hospital beds and bed pans, to pharmaceuticals, to research into the reading and interpreting of the human DNA double helix.

On May 1, 2032, the financial world was rocked by the news that, against the ineffectual objections of several governments, an announcement was made that Harvestman Agricultural Combine, the Sutton Group, and GenMedico had merged. The resulting entity was too big to fit into any known category or fall under any existing label like "corporation" or "conglomerate." It had enough assets to buy most nations on Earth. It was known simply as HSG. The big question on the lips of many people, in the financial world, in government, and amongst ordinary citizenry, was, "Why?" After the flurry of changes in 2032, the answer would not come for four years.

Chapter Two
The Project Begins

The answer to the question of why HAC, the Sutton Group, and GenMedico had merged was far more surprising than the merger itself. The powers behind the three companies had pooled their resources to create a project of hard-to-grasp magnitude and still-unknown purpose. On December 12th of 2036 HSG launched a ship on a trajectory to Mercury. The launch took place from a location in the Crazy Mountains of Montana. The United States government protested vehemently, but the legal branch of HSG, itself large enough to overwhelm any government, promptly produced a handful of permits and legal briefs. The United States government could do nothing except point fingers, fling mud, and shout loudly within its own halls.

When the unmanned ship approached Mercury, it launched a robotic probe. It had to land on the terminator -- the constantly-shifting line between the icy dark of night and the scorching light of day -- exactly, to avoid fusion or freezing of its components. Exact timing was required; exact timing was attained. Immediately upon landing, the probe quickly began digging downward. It did not stop until it was down almost half a kilometer, which was the depth judged to keep the probe safe from the temperatures of the surface. As it dug down, the tunnel above it collapsed. It was incapable of experiencing concern, but would not have been concerned by the collapse, even if it held that ability, as it was destined to remain below Mercury's surface indefinitely, and had a shell designed to withstand intense weights and pressures. When it had reached the prescribed depth, it began analyzing the surrounding rock and other material, and sending its results back to Earth using a small but powerful pulse-maser. When the researchers back at HSG received the encrypted telemetry, they smiled.

After the probe finished sampling and sending telemetry, it received the green light, from HSG, to proceed to Phase Two of its mission. It began fusing rock around it, slowly but steadily forming a dome-shaped layer of very hard, smooth rock-glass, not unlike obsidian or volcanic glass. It left one circular hole, twelve meters in diameter. It finished ahead of schedule, albeit only minutes ahead, and sent a pulse-maser signal Earthward.

Starting in February of 2037, HSG launched an entire flotilla of unmanned rockets toward Mercury. One misfired and landed in the middle of a rich actor's Montana ranch. He was promptly, and generously, compensated for the disfigurement of his land and the deaths of four beefalo (cattle-buffalo hybrids, designed ironically by HSG). The rest of the rockets reached orbit around Mercury, dropping robotic probes in a rain of expensive gadgetry.

The robotic probes that safely landed on the surface, erected a parabolic mirror umbrella to ward off some of the searing sunlight, and then began burrowing. As they tunneled down, they laid a track that allowed sand and rock to be deposited up on the surface. Deeper and deeper they went, until they were four hundred meters down. Twelve shafts went down. At the bottom of each shaft, the robotic probe began excavating out a cavern, still railroading the debris up through the chimneys. These caverns were eventually nicknamed the Pits.

One rocket carried a different mechanism, as it had a different mission. It landed where the original HSG probe had landed, followed its path downward, leaving an umbrella and a track system behind. When it reached the circular opening in the dome, it continued on, and began creating an enormous cavern, eating away all material using a recently-patented cool-fusion torch. This one would eventually be nicknamed the Apple's Core.

Repeated requests to HSG regarding some explanation of what they were doing met with the repeated statement: "HSG will provide a press release at a later date, describing the nature and purpose of its current endeavors."

Chapter Three
The Next Round

On the third day of June in 2038, HSG launched its first manned mission. There was no crew, as the ship was completely robotic. There were two passengers: Bill and Jana Gottfried. Bill was an artist who specialized in sculpting rock. Jana was a dress and costume designer. The world wondered, and the media demanded to know, why these two particular people were going to Mercury. HSG made no reply to all inquiries.

On the eighth of August in 2038, HSG launched another rocket that was crewed by robotics alone, but carried passengers. This time, there were twelve passengers. This time, inquiries to HSG, regarding what was going on, met with the announcement: "On August 24, 2038, HSG staff will hold a press conference to update the public about its current projects."

On August 24, 2038, at 12:12 PM, a

spokesperson for HSG, named Lana Montague, conducted a brief press conference, with the written preamble that no questions would be taken after the statement from Ms. Montague. The transcript of the HSG statement read by Ms. Montague:

"As has been widely reported in the media, and confirmed by astronomers, HSG has begun a space program. The purpose of this program is neither conquest, claiming of territory, resource-seeking, nor exploration. Our company has chosen to undertake an ambitious research program in the medical arena. Our goals are lofty, and we hope the results will one day benefit all of humankind. However, the research being planned is potentially extremely dangerous, as well as requiring levels of containment not possible on Earth. We therefore chose to locate this research to sub-surface units on Mercury, where the risk of contagion is nullified by the heat, the solar radiation, and the lack of a substantial atmosphere. We do not anticipate results from this project for months, years, or possibly even decades, and we will update the public and the medical community as breakthroughs are achieved. Thank you."

Ms. Lana Montague was true to the preamble, and promptly walked off stage, despite the clamoring members of the media.

Part Two
On Mercury

Chapter Four
The Midas Factor

As the searing sun tortured the surface of Mercury, an equally tortured man grieved far below the small planet's surface. The lone man stood, sobbing, among benches covered with computers and laboratory equipment, and five dead bodies.

However, he was not alone in his plight, as eleven other people stood in eleven other isolated units. Rock stood between the units, and all the air was superheated before circulating back. Each unit only received air that it had used before, after it visited the greenhouse earmarked for that unit, for re-oxygenation. The water followed similar paths and precautions. This gave a new definition to "hermetically sealed."

The twelve men and women had come to Mercury to do highly dangerous research that could benefit all humanity and extend the lifespan of many. They had sought cures; they found death. They wanted to give others longer, healthier lives; they gave themselves immortality. But, the cost was atrocious.

The year was 2060.

Five days later, Dr. Martin Goldsmith contacted Earth, and explained to HSG personnel that their research into enhancing the human immune system had succeeded all too well, and it now appeared that direct contact with any of the twelve researchers, by another human being, would quickly result in the researcher's immune system targeting the other person as a threat, and attacking that person mercilessly and, most definitely, lethally. It also appeared that the researchers had become physically younger, healthier, and able to quickly redress just about any insult or injury to their bodies, short of incineration, beheading, or an explosion.

A journalist from a small virtual newspaper, out of suburban southern Michigan, coined the term "the Midas

Factor" as it related to the benefits and hazards now involved with the researchers on Mercury, and the term became used widely in short order.

Chapter Five
Allocation of Tasks

It was Thursday evening. The Sages, living underground, had decided to ignore the concept of a Mercurial calendar, and continued to follow the calendar of Earth. Specifically, they synchronized with Eastern Standard Time in the United States. The date was August 6, 2068. They had not name themselves Sages, but had succumbed to the vox populi of Earth, who had taken to the term, just as they had "the Midas Factor" and "the Pits." Each Sage had created a statement against total conformity with Earth terminology related to them, by giving themselves new last names, to honor twelve great scientific minds in Earth history.

Thursday evening meant the weekly virtual conference of the Sages. It meant that the twelve immortal humans had a chance to gossip, gripe, update each other, argue the merits of new requests and prioritize those tasks that were voted as Accepted, and debate whom should do which task.

The task idea had arisen about a year after the twelve researchers simultaneously exposed themselves to a new variant of a product they were creating: nanotechnology-enhanced immune system enhancers. They suddenly had to come face-to-face with the daunting prospect of a potentially-eternal life of isolation. What does one do with hundreds, thousands, and possibly millions of years to fill? They came up with the concept of accepting requests from Earth to solve problems in the scientific realm. But, which tasks? Hence, the Thursday meetings.

Because of the nature of the Sages, they could never meet each other, or anyone else, in person. They had designed an elaborate holographic projection system, though, that simulated them being together.

This concept had been played with in fiction for well over a hundred year. It served their purposes.

Part Three
The Trip

Chapter Six
Outward Bound

The ship that slipped silently through space toward the limn of the sun represented the latest in human technology, although few would call it beautiful. The fore section, which contained the passenger compartment, the bridge, and the crew quarters, looked like a soup can. Closer inspection would reveal that the soup can was spinning rapidly to create artificial gravity along the inside of the "can". Just aft of the soup can was a smaller can, which was not spinning. This held the landing craft and escape pods, which had never been used and, with some luck, would never be needed. Aft of the small can was a longer, thinner cylinder that contained the robots and equipment necessary for emergency external repairs. This cylinder was not spinning. Further aft yet was a large, backward-facing bell, which was the shielding for the fusion fires it contained. During acceleration, as the ship was currently undergoing, alternating, patterned brilliant explosions of nuclear fire periodically erupted inside the bell and propelled the ship forward. Such a ship was usually used for Very Important Persons, because of its sophistication and comfort, not to mention cost, or for critical medical/rescue missions, because of its speed. The current mission of the Intrepid was not usual. Besides the four crew members (pilot, co-pilot, communications officer, and engineer), there were only six passengers, and none of them knew anything about doctoring or would have been recognized on the Virtual News Net.

    A young couple sat up front and did not interact with the other four passengers. Their self-imposed isolation was understandable given that they had chosen to replace the Caretakers on Mercury, which would mean a minimum of twenty years without any actual human contact (other than with each other). As usual, a married but infertile couple had been chosen, with both having careers that were compatible with isolation. Thomas Marchond, a stocky man with jet-black hair that he wore artistically long, was a virtual author who could compose his audio-visual sonatas and preferred solitude to allow his creative forces to go where they would. His latest work, an artistic attack on the history of slavery, was entitled "Egregious." Lynnette Marchond, was a tall statuesque blonde who was physically impressive from twenty feet away, but whose beauty became less apparent at close range. Ms. Marchond was a geological engineer for whom the strange composition of Mercury would be a treasure trove of learning for her two decades in residence.

The other four, who sat in the back of the thirty-seat passenger compartment, were all genetically-engineered Security Specialists. Gaston Lefevre came from the Lascaux School, which emphasized size and strength in its breeding and training programs. Lascaux Specialists were easily recognizable, as they were seldom under two meters tall and seldom weighed less than one hundred kilograms. Gaston, at two hundred ten centimeters tall and one hundred four kilograms, was no exception. What was exceptional about him was that he had scored a +2.1 Intelligence Factor, which was above the standard for Lascaux Specialists, who were not known for their clever wit and conversation.

 Celeste Cavanaugh came from the Honduras School, which was generally considered to be the "flip-side" of the Lascaux School. Honduran Specialists were generally small, fast, very bright, and known for their stealth. When a Honduran solved a case, the criminal usually did not know the Honduran was on the trail until he or she had hand-cuffs on. Celeste stood one hundred fifty-seven centimeters and weighed forty-three kilos. She also held black belts in four different martial arts, and her Intelligence Factor was rumored to exceed +3.0. She had a charming smile and casual style of conversing that often disarmed the listener.

She was very dangerous.

Michael Klein was from the Oxford School, where the perfect solution to a crime would be characterized by the investigator never leaving the scene of the crime. The joke was that Oxfords always carried sleeping-bags because they camped out at crime scenes. At eighty-four, Michael was near retirement, and he had not relished the summons from the Sages, no matter how much of an honor it represented.

Sean Aldred had been bred and raised at the Kyle Academy in Honor, Michigan. While Michael was near retirement, and Gaston and Celeste were seasoned veterans with impressive catch-and-prosecute records, Sean was a novice and could not figure out how he had ended up in the group. His Factor Scores were all high, although none of them were above 2.7 and his Intelligence Factor was rumored to be below two. He knew that rumor was false, but not by much.

Two days earlier, the four Specialists had been summoned from the field and told that they had been called to Mercury by the Sages. For all of them, this summons had been totally unexpected, as no one could remember the Sages ever requesting humans to come to Mercury, other than the Caretakers. Even the Caretakers were but aloofly tolerated. The summons was not made known to the public, and the Specialists had been told at their initial briefings that, whether they chose to accept the summons or not, they were to keep it in absolute confidence, with the penalty for breaking that confidence being death. They had accepted, with varying degrees of enthusiasm. A rumor had circulated at the Boulder Spaceport that a fifth Specialist had declined the summons, but the briefing team had refused to respond to questions in that area.

The first two days of the trip had consisted of a cycle of sleeping, lectures on the history of the Sages, more lectures, a short sleep period, another lecture. The lectures were either given by the incoming Caretakers, the Marchonds, or were video presentations from a Professor Theodore Saint-Germain of Newfoundland, who specialized in the history of science.

When the acceleration blasts were finally done, they were served a feast. Eating much of anything would have been nearly impossible during acceleration, as fusion-blasts produced speed but not a smooth ride. The food was plentiful and more than passable, and five of the six passengers went to sleep soon after the meal. Sean could not get to sleep, and eventually went forward to request a com-link to Earth. The Engineer reluctantly approved the request, and Sean spoke with Peter Carson, his mentor at the Kyle Academy. Peter had agreed to try to find out why Sean had been chosen for this mission (without knowing what the mission was or even where Sean was going), and Sean wanted to check if he had made any progress. Peter sounded irritated when he told Sean that he had no information for him, and Sean wondered if this was because he had awakened Peter, or because Peter did not like being kept in the dark, or simply because it bothered Peter to not be able to find out something. Sean went back to his seat, strapped himself in, and reclined. He had six more days to ponder his situation, and he knew it was unlikely that he would have an answer until the Sages chose to reveal it.

Celeste Cavanaugh, who had apparently been unable to stay asleep -- or had feigned sleep to begin with -- approached Sean. This was not surprising, as the Honduran Specialists were known for using their charm and social skills to wheedle information from people without the subject being aware that an interrogation was under way. Sean decided to take the initiative. "In all those lectures, they really did not tell us anything most people do not already know, did they?"

Celeste paused a fraction of a second, telling Sean that she had been primed to initiate the conversation, but she recovered quickly. "Very true. They gave us all the basic facts about the twelve biomedical engineering researchers, who became the

Sages, the elaborate safety precautions to prevent the spread, from unit to unit, of the bio-nanotechnology, the disastrous events of 2160, and the role of the Sages since then. But, there was nothing to hint at why we were summoned. They also said little about the other people who have used their wealth to join the Sages."

"Right. We are no closer to knowing why anyone was summoned, or why we, in particular, were chosen. Except, we are thousands of kilometers closer."

Having learned nothing from each other, but Celeste receiving the message that Sean was not interested in being subtly interrogated, the two went to sleep.

When they awoke the next "day", which was defined by the ship's internal lighting, acceleration was fully finished and weightlessness would have ruled, had it not been for the artificial gravity. Their breakfast still came out of tubes and straws instead of off of plates, and using the toilet became an adventure, as the spin-induced gravity was not strong. Of the six passengers, only Michael Klein had been in space before, and he was not free with advice. The others did their best and, once they had survived breakfast and other morning rituals, they all searched for something to do. Sean activated his portable computer and studied Mercury. Astronomy had never been a real interest of his, but now necessity became the mother of curiosity.

Suddenly, he whistled to get everyone's attention. "Mr. and Mrs. Marchond, were you supposed to come to Mercury now?"

They looked at him with surprise as everyone else looked at him with annoyance. Mrs. Marchond answered, "No, but how did you know?"

Now, the others began to look more curious than annoyed. This time, Sean liked being in the spotlight, which was unusual for him (both being there and liking it). "Because Mercury is nowhere near perigee. If this trip had been pre-planned, we would have waited for perigee, when Mercury and Earth are only ninety-two million kilometers apart. Right now, they're one hundred seventy million kilometers apart. I think we're facing some type of emergency or deadline."

Michael Klein was back to being annoyed. "What kind of emergency could the Sages have?"

Celeste shook her head. "The kind we won't like, I'll bet."

That brief conversation was the only thing interesting that occurred for the rest of the trip. They played cards, which is difficult but not impossible in free-fall, and they slept a lot. They studied their portable computers and compared hardware and software. They talked sports. They wrote letters to loved ones and friends. They even flirted with one another, although this embarrassed Sean and he tried to avoid it. In short, they were bored.

When the Intrepid reached its closest point to Mercury, the six passengers were alerted to head toward the center of the forward cylinder, where the artificial gravity of the spinning quickly diminished to nothing. They crawled back out of the large can and into the small can, where they boarded the landing craft. The landing craft looked like a small hockey puck (passenger compartment) atop a larger hockey puck (engines and landing gear). When the six passengers and the Intrepid's landing craft copilot were belted into their seats, the side of the small can swung open and small gas explosions pushing the lander away from its mooring clamps. It drifted down toward the border between the sun-side and the dark-side of Mercury's surface, while the Intrepid continued on its swing-around orbit of the sun. It would rendezvous with the lander on the return trip; this avoided the need to decelerate.

The sun-side of Mercury reached temperatures of 810 degrees Fahrenheit, while the dark-side was a chilly -290 degrees Fahrenheit. It was only along the boundary between the two zones that humans could do anything for more than a few seconds. As the lander dropped through Mercury's almost-non-existent atmosphere of sodium and potassium, and neared the crater-pocked surface, a small metal doorway, just inside the dark-side, could be seen. The lander plopped down on top of the doorway, and the passengers climbed down through the access chute in their temperature-resistant suits and dropped in the one-third Earth-gravity onto a cushioned mat. The door above them closed, and they immediately heard the rockets of the lander blasting. It would orbit until time for rendezvous with Intrepid. The boundary between light and dark (incineration and freeze-drying) shifted slowly but inexorably, and the lander had to leave immediately. The next sound was the sighing of the airlock as the room they were in pressurized.

Part Four
Belowground

Chapter Seven
Caretakers' Cottage

The couple who met the passengers of the Intrepid were the current Caretakers of Mercury, whom the Marchond's were replacing. They appeared to be in their eighties, but they both looked to be in good health and good spirits.

"Welcome to Mercury! We were not able to prepare a proper welcome, as we were not told of your impending arrival until an hour ago."

The man, who had done the speaking so far, nodded to the Marchonds.

"We knew you two were coming, but we didn't expect you for another four months or so. It's Peter and Susan Allister, is it not?" The man smiled and extended his hand to Thomas Marchond, whose face was quickly reddening.

"Actually, sir, the Allisters were

disqualified and we are Thomas and Lynnette Marchond."

The older man and woman both frowned fleetingly, but then recovered their good cheer. The woman spoke now.

"I'm Melissa Goodwright and this is my husband of fifty-six years, David. Welcome to our home, which I hope will soon feel like is be your temporary new home. We will stay on until the regular supply ship comes in four months, which will give us plenty of time to help you get acclimated. We will have plenty of room, as there are guest cottages, although they are seldom used. Speaking of climate, though, we best continue our introductions as we head toward the habitat zone. It will be getting toasty in here fairly soon."

For the next fifteen or twenty minutes, the group strolled quickly but quietly through a steadily descending maze of tunnels, using the ever-present hand-railings to speed up their pace in the low gravity. They chatted idly about nothing of consequence. The smooth gray tunnel walls and floors formed a tube and became monotonous, with fluorescent overhead lighting keeping the maze from being downright dreary.

The tunnel suddenly leveled out and ended at what had once been an undecorated metal airlock door. Above the doorway, someone had carefully painted "Caretakers' Domain" in Old English letters, with ivy and holly painted to weave around the lettering. Melissa Goodwright pointed to the artwork, which measured three meters across and a meter high, "That's David's handiwork. He did that thirty-seven years ago, right after we arrived. With no wind and low humidity, and occasional touch-ups, it still looks fresh."

Mr. Goodwright went to the airlock controls and placed his hand over the palm-reader. The green light flashed on and the door slid silently open. The small group walked through, and the airlock door slid just as quietly closed behind them.

The view on the other side of the airlock created a contrast almost as great as the temperature swings of Mercury. The group walked along a narrow dirt path through a hilly, wooded area, with birds singing and a beautiful blue sky with the sun shining above. The newcomers just gaped as they walked, while Mr. and Mrs. Goodwright smiled whenever they glanced at their guests. After a few minutes of letting them admire the view, Mr. Goodwright chuckled and said, "We were astounded when we first saw it, too. The Sages have created technology that is almost beyond belief. You are looking at an elaborate composite of natural cave attributes, artificially sculpted features, holographic imaging, and climatic manipulation. The plants and animals are real, and the light that you experience does not come from the 'sun' that you see in this 'sky' but is actual sunlight brought here via a set of cleverly placed mirrored conduits. It is filtered so as to be not too harsh, and the radiation is somehow removed. We are not scientifically-minded, but Sage Reimann explained it to us soon after our arrival."

The dirt path eventually switched to a cobblestone walkway as the forest opened up to a clearing. An elaborate flower garden filled the air with a mixture or fragrances, and the cobblestones ended at the porch of a quaint, Alpine-style cottage. The Goodwrights led their guests into the cottage, and they found themselves in a house where every feature bespoke of northern European influence.

Melissa Goodwright turned to her guests and said, "Would you care to freshen up, or for a snack, before we head for the briefing room?"

Several guests took her "freshen up" offer. Sean Aldred wandered the edges of the sitting room, briefly examining the many knick-knacks and photographs. When everyone was ready, the Goodwrights led their guests down a narrow, winding, wooden staircase. Sean felt like he was headed for his great-grandmother's Michigan basement, where she had kept all of her home-canned fruits and vegetables. At the bottom of the stairway, they encountered a creaky wooden door, or at least what appeared to be a creaky wooden door. Sean looked at the back of the door after going through, and the other side looked like a modern aluminum-carbon-fiber door.

When he turned back around, he saw that this was certainly NOT his great-grandmother's basement. His fellow guests all had the same, surprised expression on their faces as they examined the ultra-modern yet somehow cozy conference room, which was complete with three holographic ports and a five-meter display wall-screen. The floor sloped, and the overall appearance was that of a thirty-seat amphitheater-style classroom that all of the guests had experienced in one graduate school or another.

The Goodwrights bade their guests to seat themselves, and Mr. Goodwright took his place at the podium in front of the wall-screen.

"Although we have two very different groups with different purposes here, the same orientation lecture can apply to everyone. I'll start with a basic overview of the history of our little domain, which will contain some facts about Mercury and its residents that are no longer widely discussed and, in my estimation, have been forgotten by many."

"In 2024, a research facility on the dark side of the moon was conducting experiments into nano-technology. You might not have heard this term before, as the results of the experiment held on the moon created a very negative connotation for nano-technology. When several of the researchers were killed during experiments of various types, security and containment concerns triggered the shutting down of the facility. By then, the moon was becoming more populated, and it was deemed to no longer be a good location for such research.

"Eventually, this facility was founded. One of the researchers, Dr. Martin Goodall, became infested, in 2060, with nanites, which are microscopic machines, built atom-by-atom, and designed to interact with chemical compounds or organic chemical systems. Overnight, the elderly Dr. Goodall de-aged approximately fifty years, lost all symptoms of his arthritis and hypertension, developed a photographic memory, and became immune to every disease known to man. Unfortunately, the nanites that inhabited his body identified Dr. Goodall's assistants as biological threats to their host, probably because the other researchers each carried a host of benign bacteria and other parasites. Dr. Goodall's newly-enhanced immune system extended itself through the atmosphere and destroyed every other person in his section of the facility. Dr. Goodall's new immune system identified any living tissue with DNA different from Dr. Goodall's as a health threat to be eliminated.

"Like any good researcher, Dr. Goodall made detailed notes and shared these with several fellow nano-technology researchers. Although news of the disaster was kept from the general public for a while, some of the facts began to leak out. Four other researchers here isolated themselves and infested themselves with nanites, in direct opposition to the rules of their research sponsors. They all experienced benefits similar to Dr. Goodall's. These benefits include an apparent stoppage of the natural aging process and greatly enhanced memory and cognitive processes. However, when two of these researchers experimented with interpersonal contact with each other, their immune systems went to war, and both were dead within an hour. That left ten researchers here, three of whom were nanite-affected.

"Despite the isolation required by nanite-enhanced body chemistry, the remaining seven researchers, along with fourteen wealthy research sponsors who learned of the effects of nano-technology on human body chemistry, chose to infest themselves. The twenty-four resulting nanite-humans still show no signs of aging. Each individual has remained completely isolated since then, with elaborate climate control to protect each other, and with advanced holographic communication systems to provide social contact.

"In 2064, these individuals, who by then were known as 'the Sages,' further developed this facility, and the Caretakers domain was also improved. The Sages have devoted their lives to the advancement of human knowledge and technology, and have shared this knowledge with Earth in exchange for the few raw materials they need to survive here, and the constant presence of at least two non-nanite humans to act as Caretakers."

David Goodwright flipped a switch on his podium, and the wall-screen lit up to show a display of the Mercury base from an aerial view. "As this simulation proceeds, it will reveal to you the schematics of this base from the surface down. You will see that each of the Sages has his or her own cell, which is actually a luxurious but completely self-contained and atmospherically-isolated apartment, with adjacent research laboratories. There are interconnecting tunnels, but they are kept in high-temperature vacuum to insure isolation and containment of the nanites. Robots do all repair work, with each cell having its own set of robots that never come into physical contact with each other or with any human except the Sage it serves.

"This system ran perfectly until three weeks ago when, after years of no significant problems at this base, one of the Sages was found dead by his robot team." David Goodwright paused to let the significance of this statement sink in. He sighed and said, "Now you know why scheduling changes were made and why four of Earth's top Specialists, hand-picked by the remaining Sages, were invited here. I will now field basic questions, but any significant information about the Sages, beyond what I have already said, will have to be provided by them. They have almost all agreed to make themselves available to all of you on an unlimited basis until the mystery of Sage Newton's death is resolved."

Sean jumped on the words "almost all."

"What do you mean by 'almost all' of the Sages?" The other three Specialists were nodding their approval of the question while frowning at Sean for beating them to it.

David Goodwright shrugged and answered with a genuinely puzzled expression on his face, "My wife and I do not know why Sage Goodall is refusing all communication, and the other Sages claim ignorance in the matter as well. Sage Goodall's robot team assures us that the Sage is alive and well."

Gaston Lefevre spoke up. "What can you tell us about the crime scene and the nature of the Sage's death?"

David Goodwright shook his head. "I was told to expect such inquiries and specifically instructed not to discuss the crime scene or the body with you." There was a tone of irritation in his voice, but no one could tell whether this was directed at Lefevre or at the "instructions" the old gentleman had received. Mr. Goodwright glanced at his watch and added, "Sage Reimann is scheduled to make a holographic appearance here in about ten minutes, and I expect that he will answer many of those questions. Also, you are requested to decide how long you want your initial interviews with each Sage to be, so that they can work out a schedule. At this time, I intend to retire for dinner. Dinner will be available for all of you after the audience. The Sage will appear over there." David Goodwright pointed at a holographic port to his right, which was simply a circle drawn on the floor in red, with a one-meter-wide, two-meter-long cylinder suspended from the ceiling directly above it. Mr. Goodwright quickly and quietly made his exit.

*   *   *   *   *

At the appointed time, the area above the circle on the floor shimmered, and the image of a man crystallized in the holographic port. The man looked to be eighteen to twenty years old, and he had medium-length dark brown hair and startlingly blue eyes. He appeared seated in a comfortable-looking arm-chair. He glanced at his audience, shook his head in disgust, and said curtly, "This audience is meant only for the four Specialists. Will the Caretakers-to-be please excuse themselves; I will meet with you two tomorrow."

The Marchonds looked at each other, and then quickly exited. The Sage covered his face with his hands for a second, and then looked at his remaining audience. The expression on his face had changed completely; he now looked benevolent and kindly, instead of stern and condescending. "I am the Sage Reimann. My name was originally Steven Galbraith, and I am of the sub-group called the Academics, as I was one of the Sages who was a researcher before choosing infestation and isolation. I am here to begin answering your questions regarding the death of Sage Newton, who was also an Academic." He spread his hands before him, palms up, in a gesture of invitation.

Celeste Cavanaugh jumped at that invitation. "I know this might be difficult for you, but please describe the body as it was found."

Sage Reimann nodded. "A good place to begin. We, of course, have extensive holographic recordings of the body made within a few minutes of the discovery. For all intents and purposes, the body appears to have exploded from several internal locations simultaneously. You should know that this manner of death is identical to the deaths of my early colleagues who experimented with interpersonal contact after accepting co-existence with nanites."

Gaston Lefevre took his turn. "Could the integrity of Sage Newton's cell have been breached, allowing contact with nanites from one of the other Sages?"

Again Sage Reimann nodded and smiled faintly. "A logical next question, except if we had discovered that, we would hardly have needed to summon you. No, there is no evidence of non-Newton nanites in Sage Newton's cell. Also, if the integrity of his cell had been breached, his nanites would have affected at least one other Sage -

the one whose nanites had killed Sage Newton, if that had indeed been the case. Next question."

Sean Aldred was beginning to feel that the Specialists were being tested as much as they were being briefed. However, there was no choice but to go along with whatever was happening. "Is there anything in early Sage history wherein a Sage died under similar circumstances, other than by contact with another Sage?"

Sage Reimann briefly looked as if Sean had slapped his face. He recovered quickly and answered briefly and curtly, "No. No Sage has ever died, except for the first few who tried interpersonal contact. Next question."

If this were some kind of test, Sean felt he had just lost points. Everyone looked at Michael Klein, as it was now his turn. His eyes were closed, but he knew somehow that everyone was looking at him. He made a small wave gesture with his hand, ending up by pointing at Celeste. He had decided to pass.

Celeste was ready with another question. "Aren't the Sages monitored in case of a mishap of some kind?"

For the first time, Sage Reimann appeared pleasantly startled by a question. "No, there has been no need. The nanites repair minor and even somewhat significant injuries with a rapidity that is astonishing, and each of the Sage cells contains a medical robot unit that is activated by the faintest request for help from its Sage. Let me demonstrate." Sage Reimann reached outside the scope of the holographic image being projected and retrieved a knife. He seemed to have planned for this demonstration. He quickly cut his left little finger almost off, and then held up his initially-gushing hand for display. With a speed that was truly astounding, the bleeding slowed and stopped, as the cut gradually narrowed and vanished. Despite the obvious lack of need for aid, a robot had immediately appeared, just behind the sage, with a suture tray ready. Sage Reimann smiled. "Either Sage Newton had no time to make such a request, or he chose not to."

Sean jumped in out of turn, which produced an annoyed look on Gaston Lefevre's face. "Could this have been a suicide?"

Again, Sean caused Sage Reimann to briefly lose his composure, although the signs were very subtle - a clenching of one fist and a tightening of the muscles around the jaw. The look that Reimann gave Sean made the young man shudder, and the Sage's response was exceptionally brief: "No."

To Gaston's credit, he did not let his transient annoyance at Sean stand in the way of good investigative procedure. "Why not?"

That simple question, logical and appropriate though it was to the situation, startled the other Specialists; the Sages had become almost mythical and somewhat godlike to the people of Earth, and Gaston Lefevre had just come close to calling a Sage a liar. Reimann showed more restraint, as if acknowledging that this question, however impertinent it might be, was a logical expectation.

"Our past and current research shows no way that a Sage could produce the observed manner of death on himself without physical contact with body-alien nanites. We are at a loss to explain this death."

Michael Klein finally spoke up. "The robots who serve the Sages never switch teams?"

This question must have been one Reimann had anticipated, as he smiled and said, "No. Robot-transported nanite contamination has been ruled out. However, it was a logical possibility."

Sean thought to himself that Michael Klein probably had an "A" on this exam so far, with Gaston and Celeste earning B's and himself earning a "D-". If this really were a test, it was time for him to come up with a good question. "What was the nature of Sage Newton's relationships with the other Sages?"

Sage Reimann stared at Sean for

several seconds before answering, but this pause seemed to be a product of contemplation instead of anger. "If you are implying the possibility of murder, then non-Newton nanites would be present in the body, and I have already stated that no evidence of other-Sage infestation has been found."

Sean wasn't ready to let go. "Yes, but given the many technological marvels your people have produced for humanity, as well as here on Mercury, I feel unable to say what would be beyond the ability of a Sage. Perhaps, contamination occurred, but the scene and the body were then decontaminated, or it was achieved via a manner I could not conceive."

Everyone looked at him, and Sean knew that he had just raised his grade considerably. Sage Reimann finally said, "I suppose that will have to be one of your avenues of investigation here."

Celeste knew they were running out of time in this interview, so she jumped in quickly. "Have you been able to definitely rule out foul play from an outside agent?"

Sage Reimann almost jumped. "Outside? What do you mean?"

"There are factions on Earth who worship the Sages as deities. Whenever humans have worshipped anything or anyone, there have been counter-groups. A group calling themselves the 'Scientific Rationalists' have lately been acting in a very militant and, in my opinion, non-rational manner, including engaging in persecution of those who worship you, harassing travelers and ships headed toward Mercury, and spreading propaganda suggesting that the Sages have all died off and the government is keeping the story of your existence alive as a way to maintain stability. Could a radical member of such a group have gotten to Mercury, killed Sage Newton, and then escaped?"

Sage Newton shrugged. "I had not even considered that possibility. Feel free to investigate that avenue, but I don't think it will be a fruitful endeavor. As I have another commitment in three minutes, I need to conclude this interview. However, if you write down your scheduling requests, the Sages will arrange it so that each of you can interview each of us in the next week, for however long you desire. The Sages have agreed that no questions will go unanswered, so feel free to pry away." The hologram of Sage Reimann smiled, and then vanished. The audience was clearly over.

Chapter Eight
Legwork

The four Specialists just looked at each other for a minute after the Sage disappeared. Michael Klein stood up, stretched, and walked out of the conference room without saying a word. Sean took the initiative. "At least in the beginning, does either of you want to meet to discuss preliminary theories?"

Celeste answered first. "I wouldn't mind a powwow. How about we eat that dinner Mr. Goodwright mentioned, check out our quarters, and then meet one hour after eating?"

Gaston nodded. "That sounds good to me too."

Sean smiled. "One hour after dinner it is, then. Should we invite Klein?"

Celeste laughed. "You can try, but his quick, silent exit, and the reputation of the Oxfords, suggest that you won't have much luck."

Sean did approach Michael Klein, who sat in the yoga position on the floor in the hallway outside the conference-room door, but Klein appeared to be in a trance and did not respond in any way. Sean was suspicious about the depth of the "trance" however and guessed that Klein had been eavesdropping on the conversation of the other Specialists.

By the time Sean had given up on getting Klein to respond and had caught up with Gaston and Celeste, the other two had already approached Mrs. Goodwright and had been seated for dinner. The meal was sumptuous and consisted of roast turkey, cranberry sauce, mashed potatoes enhanced with smoked gouda cheese, and an elaborate salad with dried cherries and golden raisins, with a lime-mint vinaigrette dressing. Afterward, they were given directions to their quarters, which were in the same environment as the cottage, but not in the cottage itself.

The three followed the directions the Goodwrights had provided and sauntered through the warm "afternoon sunshine" that reigned "outside" and followed a narrow winding dirt path through the woods that led to a small clearing holding half a dozen rustic cabins. Each cabin had a main room with a table, chairs, a computer terminal built into one wall, and a kitchen nook built into the opposite wall; the rest of the cabin consisted of a small bedroom with a small but comfortable cot and a small but fully-equipped bathroom. After they had each taken a cabin and went in to briefly explore and dump off their luggage, they gathered in the clearing between the cabins. They built a small fire, as "dusk" did not appear to be far off.

Once the fire was going well, Sean started the conversation. "I see four possibilities: suicide, death by weird but natural causes, murder by an outside agent or agents, and murder by one or more of the other Sages. Reimann acts as if none of these is possible but, the fact remains that Sage Newton is dead."

Celeste had a frown on her face. "What do you mean by 'death by weird but natural causes'?"

"No human has ever lived as long as the Sages have lived, which means that we have no idea what disease processes might be possible. Perhaps something finally, catastrophically, and explosively overcame the tremendous immune system of Sage Newton. The tighter a system is controlled, the more dramatic will be the failure. The natural-causes theory is probably the weakest, as the manner of death is reportedly consistent with alien-nanite infection, but that doesn't mean it can be ruled out."

Celeste scowled at Sean. "You don't need to lecture me on rule-out principles, junior. However, I must admit that I had not thought of the natural-causes possibility and I also agree that it should be kept in mind as a low-probability option."

Gaston tossed a twig into the fire. "Of the other three theories, they all seem equally plausible and equally unlikely. While we might not know enough about Sage technology to say with certainty that another Sage could or could not have contaminated Newton and then wiped any trace of contamination, Reimann seemed surprised by the suggestion. If that ability was within the realm of possibility and Reimann knew about it, he might not have seemed so surprised. From what I saw of the surface, I also think that it would be almost impossible for someone to get into this complex unannounced. Suicide is the possibility we know the least about. I wonder if a Sage has ever contemplated suicide before, or even made an attempt."

Sean nodded. "I bet their computer system could give some kind of answer to that. Immortality, or assumed immortality, might have become tedious and depressing to Newton. However, I would assume that the Sages would not have invited us here if they thought that suicide or murder by another Sage were anything but remote possibilities. We must remember that, while the Sages were not trained as Specialists, they are all extremely intelligent and the Academic sub-group is well-versed in scientific method. They must have tried very hard to solve this mystery before allowing outsiders to know what has happened."

Celeste nodded. "I was thinking along those lines during the interview with Reimann. It really is astonishing that the Sages could not solve this mystery and that they were willing to call us in. It's my guess that this is the reason why Sage Goodall has made himself incommunicado. I would also think that he has some status within the Sages as their founder, and he probably feels some parental-like guilt over Newton's death."

Gaston yawned and said, "I wish we

had some marshmallows to roast over this fire. I've never done that and, for some reason, it always sounded wonderful to me."

A small service robot suddenly appeared from behind one of the cabins, approached Gaston Lefevre, and handed him a plastic bag filled with large marshmallows, and three metal skewers. Gaston smiled and thanked the robot, who made no response but left quietly. Gaston then turned back to the Sean and Celeste. "I guess we get the royal treatment while we're here." He skewered a marshmallow and stuck it into the fire. It melted and fell in. Sean and Celeste suppressed giggles. Gaston's second attempt met with greater success.

The other two also made attempts at roasting marshmallows, but they lost a total of five before Celeste was able to produce a nice brown one. She burnt her lip on it, but eventually enjoyed it greatly. They stopped talking about the Sages, and spent almost an hour roasting marshmallows and discussing the many things they had missed out on because of their unusual childhoods in the

Specialist Academies. They then retired to their respective cabins.

Sean sat down before his computer terminal and said, "Please activate."

The screen glowed and a soothing, asexual voice said, "How may I help you, Mr. Aldred?"

"First of all, please call me Sean. I imagine that you and I will be having many a conversation in the coming weeks, and I am not comfortable with formalities. I would like anything you have on suicidal statements, suicidal gestures, suicide attempts, and evidence of suicidal ideation displayed by any Sage in their history."

"Very good, Sean. That will take a few minutes to access and collate. Would you like me to assume a male or female persona when we interact?"

Sean was startled by the question, as the computers at the Academy had all been gender-neutral, but after brief contemplation, he said, "I have lived a sheltered life when it comes to social interaction, and I think that I would be more comfortable if you assume a male persona. I have had much more interaction with males than with females, and I am more accustomed to it."

A friendly, cheerful, non-accented male voice answered, "Then male it will be. A thorough review of Sage history indicates nothing that could definitely be called a suicide attempt. All of the Sages, as they grew more and more comfortable with their healing/immune systems, have experimented with testing its capacity by self-mutilating. I believe you saw an example of this in your interview with Sage Reimann. Sage Newton, if anything, had been somewhat less adventurous in his experimentation than some of the other Sages. For example, he has never amputated any limbs, as have some of the others."

Sean was impressed with the computer's anticipation of his wish to focus on Newton, and appalled that some of the Sages had gone as far as amputating limbs just be able to observe the re-growth process. He guessed that this was somewhat logical, given the research background of some of the Sages, but it was still unsettling to consider.

The computer continued, "Many of the Sages have discussed suicide, but these discussions have generally been of an intellectually speculative nature, as in 'I wonder if decapitation would cause death or if the nanites would somehow meet that challenge.'"

The computer's voice had changed for the last sentence, and Sean was startled. "Whose voice was that for the quote?"

"I was quoting Sage Copernicus, and I used his voice."

Sean realized that he knew little about the individual Sages. "Please print out a list of the Sages, including their names, birthdates, places of birth, and one-paragraph pre-Sage biographies."

The computer quickly complied, and then continued its narration of the history of suicidal issues for the Sages. "Sage Copernicus and Sage Lavoisier have discussed, with each other, the possibility of someday engaging in a suicide pact, including ways to circumvent their robotic servants, who would go to great measures to protect their masters. There is no record of serious suicide talk from any other Sage. There is no record of any behavior by a Sage which could be interpreted as suicidal, other than the mutilation-and-healing experiments already mentioned. There are no indications of suicidal intent in any of the Sages, other than the proposed and apparently still-hypothetical suicide pact between Sages Copernicus and Lavoisier."

Sean was quiet for a few minutes, and then said, "Please explore the histories of the Sages, before they became Sages, for suicidal behavior of any kind."

The computer was quiet for thirty seconds or so, and then said, "Sage Newton attempted suicide at age fifteen and was hospitalized for seventeen days afterward. He was placed on neo-tricyclic antidepressants, which he took for one hundred eighty three days, and he met weekly with a psychologist for two hundred eighteen days following the attempt. There are no records of other suicidal behavior amongst any of the other people who became Sages."

"During the thirty days preceding Sage Newton's death, how many times did he communicate with Sage Goodall?"

"They had five holographic meetings and one voice-only communication."

Sean sat back and closed his eyes. "How unusual is it for two Sages to communicate by voice-only means?"

The computer was almost terse. "Exceptionally unusual."

Sean opened his eyes and leaned forward. "Do you have a record of that conversation?"

"That record has been erased."

"On whose authority was it erased?"

"On the authority of Sage Goodall, who is nominal sovereign of this planet."

"Do you have records of the holographic communications between Newton and Goodall?"

"Yes, I have complete recordings, and I am equipped to produce holographics at this location. Should I begin?"

Sean shook his head. "No, I am too tired. Be ready to produce those recordings, plus the holographic recording of the death scene, and holographic images of each of the Sages, tomorrow. I would like to be awakened in eight hours, please. Do you have a name?"

"No, but feel free to give me one, and I will then respond to it."

"Choose a name for yourself."

"Very well, Sean. I name myself 'Brian'."

Sean was taken aback. "'Brian' was the name of my older brother, whom I had hardly known and who died at age four, when I was about three years old."

"I know, Sean. Should I choose another name?"

Sean stared at the terminal, and then said, "No, 'Brian' is fine."

"What would you like for breakfast tomorrow, or do you want to decide that tomorrow?"

"I'll decide tomorrow - Brian. I've

found that what sounds good to me at night usually sounds very unappetizing the next morning. Good night, Brian."

"Good night, Sean. Sleep well."

"Thank you, Brian."

The screen went blank and Sean shivered. He wondered if the computer's choice of name was intended to put him off stride. However, he could think of no reason why the Sages would want him uncomfortable, other than as part of the testing that Sean suspected. He decided to forget about it for the time being, and he undressed and went to bed. He started to float off the bed once, and then remembered to use the soft restraining straps. Low gravity could be weird. As he drifted off to sleep, he knew there was something unsettling at the fringes of his consciousness that he could not quite grasp. He gave up on trying, and fell sound asleep. That night, he had vague dreams of his brother when they were very young - before Brian died and before Sean went to the Academy.

* * * * *

The next morning, Sean ate a small breakfast of rye toast, orange juice, and peaches in raspberry syrup. None of it tasted simulated. He then sat down before the computer terminal and asked, "Brian, where would you project your holographics?"

"Right behind you, Sean. The holographic projector is hidden in the ceiling to preserve the rustic decor of the cabin. What do you want to start with? The death scene?"

Sean smiled. "I guess that's as good a way to start my morning as any." He swiveled around in his chair just as an image began to materialize in the middle of the cabin. There was blood everywhere. Sean looked back at the computer. "How elaborate can you make this, Brian?"

"'Elaborate' as in how, Sean?"

"Can you make it appear that I am sitting in the middle of the room where Sage Newton died?"

The entire room shimmered and

reconfigured until Sean seemed to be sitting in the middle of a plush bedroom. Behind him was a large mirror and dresser, and in front of him was a large, four-poster brass bed. The floor was covered with teal-colored carpeting, and the walls were paneled in knotty pine. On the bed, what was left of Sage Newton was stretched out. It was hardly recognizable as a body, and Sean was repulsed by the brief thought that the bed resembled a counter at a butcher shop. Blood spattered the walls, the floor, and even the ceiling. Sean stood and walked over to the body. It looked as if it had exploded from dozens of separate internal locations, ranging from the head to the hands and feet. Nothing was left intact. Sean walked over to the door of the bedroom and found that it was locked.

"Brian, if the bedroom door was locked, how did the robotic servants find the body?"

"They knocked on the door and, when they could not get a response from Sage Newton, they used the emergency access entrance, which is located inside the closet."

Sean looked past the bed at the closet, where an array of rich clothing hung. A brief thought crossed his mind about how the Sages retained the custom of wearing clothing, despite complete isolation. Sean could see the darkness of the open access panel behind the clothes. He went over to the dresser and looked around, but found nothing but the expected: a brush, a comb, a bottle of cologne. He rifled through the drawers and found more fancy clothing and underclothing, and one photograph. "Brian, who is this a picture of?"

"That is Sage Newton's wife, who died seventy-four years ago. He used to keep the picture in a silver frame on the dresser, but he put it in the drawer over two years ago."

"Was a note found?"

"A note?"

"Yes, Brian, when the robotic team searched the cell, did they find any undelivered written or voice-recorded or holographic messages?"

"No, Sean, they found nothing like that."

"If I go through the door, can I see the rest of the cell?"

"Please give me a minute to configure the image, Sean."

A minute of silence passed, and then Brian said, "Proceed."

Sean left the bedroom and walked into the living room. A fireplace held a roaring fire, and a reproduction of Van Gogh's "Irises" hung over the mantle. A semicircular couch faced a holographic port, which was inactive. The room smelled of sandalwood incense. Off to the right, a small kitchen opened up, and it included a small mahogany dining table with two chairs. "Brian, if no one ever came in here, how come there are two chairs at the table?"

"At first, Sage Newton asked for the second chair because he said that having only one chair was a constant reminder of his isolation. Later, the second chair was often used by a robotic companion who usually joined Sage Newton for dinner. That unit, SR-Newton-14, had had no contact with Sage Newton for three days prior to the Sage's death."

"Was a gap in contact like that unusual?"

"No, Sean. Sage Newton often went days without contact with SR-Newton-14."

"Very well, Brian, end this image."

The room shimmered and Sean suddenly found himself standing in the kitchen nook of his own cabin. He made a mental note to be more careful about wandering around holographic projections, as one could easily trip over real-life objects in the space occupied by the hologram. He grabbed a glass of iced tea mixed with cranberry juice and returned to his seat by the computer terminal and said, "Please replay the holographic communications that Sage Newton had with Sage Goodall during the last month of his life."

For the next three hours, Sean sat through the five holographic conversations. They were very routine and dealt with either research proposals or administrative matters.

Apparently, Sage Goodall relied upon Sage Newton as an assistant in the running of the Mercury complex. There were no hints of depression, suicidal ideation, or anything else suspicious.

"Brian, please rapid-search the communications that Sage Newton had with other Sages during the last month of his life, and replay any mentions of death, suicide, mortality, immortality, murder, conspiracy, or anything related to any of those topics."

Sean anticipated that this would take Brian several minutes, but Brian answered almost immediately. "I anticipated that task and have already done so. Sage Newton had only one other holographic communication during his last month. He and Sage Lavoisier had dinner together once holographically, and they discussed genetic variants and hydroponics."

"There were no mentions of death-related topics?"

"None whatsoever, Sean."

"Show me a holographic image of Sage Lavoisier, please."

Sean swiveled around as a very attractive young woman's image shimmered into existence in the middle of his cabin. Sage Lavoisier was very tall and had long, flowing, auburn hair. She appeared to be having an animated conversation with someone outside the range of the holographic projector.

"Brian, is this a real-time image?"

"Yes, Sean. Sage Lavoisier is currently being interviewed by Specialist Cavanaugh. Would you like the audio on this conversation?"

"No, that will not be necessary."

Sean was accustomed to working on cases alone or with a supervisor looking over his shoulder; it would take time to get used to being part of a team. He tried to decide what to do next, but experienced another sensation of having something crucial just beyond his mental grasp. He suddenly knew that, while he did not know what to do next, he did know where to go.

"Brian, I will be gone for a while."

"Do you want lunch to take with

you?"

"No, thank you, Brian."

Chapter Nine
Up a Tree and Out on a Limb

The clearing in front of the cabin was about twenty meters across, and then the forest started. As was usual for plants growing in low-gravity situations, the trees grew tall and narrow, with elongated leaves and upward-curving branches. Sean crossed the clearing and began looking for the right tree. He followed a path other than the one that led from the Caretakers' Cottage, and he soon found an oak that was perfect. He backed up about ten meters, ran as quickly as he could in low gravity, and leapt high up into the tree. He caught hold on his first attempt, and found himself about five meters up. He climbed quickly from there, using the many thick branches as footholds and handholds. About twenty meters up, he found a good niche to curl up in, and did so. His left wrist, which he had broken in a fall from a tree at age seven, ached, but it was a familiar ache and not altogether unwelcome. That ache was often associated in his memories with him having done something strenuous and useful.

Ever since his boyhood, he had loved to climb trees, both for the thrill of the heights and because the solitude a tree gave him that created the perfect atmosphere to think. Something was very wrong here on Mercury, or at least not adding up right, and thinking is what he needed to do most. He had to try to grasp that thing in his mind that he had almost grasped twice now, and which he knew was somehow critical to the investigation of Sage Newton's death. Nothing made sense in the investigation.

The Academic Sages were incredibly bright, or at least they claimed to be, and had produced some of Mankind's greatest inventions. Many of them had backgrounds as researchers and were thoroughly versed in the scientific method. The others had been very wealthy and, while some of them might have come by that wealth through inheritance or through good fortune, Sean guessed that most of them were well acquainted with solving tough problems and getting a job done through hard work. So, why did the Sages need the four Specialists? If the Sages could not figure out this crime themselves, how could they expect the four of them to do so? And, they would be strongly motivated to keep the news of this disaster out of the public domain. This led to an unsettling thought: what would happen to the four Specialists after they had solved the mystery of Sage Newton's death? And, what about the Caretakers - out-going and in-coming - would they be trusted with the news of the disaster, especially if one or more of the other Sages were implicated?

Sean had repeatedly evaluated the plausibility of the theories they had considered to date - murder from the outside, murder from the inside, suicide, and death by natural causes - and was left more confused than ever. He agreed with Sage Reimann that murder from the outside, that is murder by an agent from Earth, the Moon, or a space station, was not possible. The chances of leaving any spaceport undetected, arriving on Mercury undetected, entering the habitat undetected, finding Sage Newton undetected, killing the Sage undetected, and escaping undetected, and without leaving a trace, were astronomically low. If the information they had been given were accurate, murder by another Sage or by one of the Caretakers was also impossible, as the murderer would also be fatally exposed.

Murder by a robot was technically a possibility, but the Three Laws of Robotics, proposed in fiction by the great science fiction writer Isaac Asimov but found to be so thoroughly necessary to human-robot interaction that they were universally incorporated into robots, made the robots very low-probability suspects. After all, the First Law of Robotics forbade a robot from harming a human being or, by inaction, allowing a human being to come to harm. That meant that a robot could not kill a human or allow a human to kill himself or do something very risky in the robot's presence. While the Second Law of Robotics stated that robots must obey human beings, it included a caveat that this Second Law was superseded by the First Law, making it impossible for a robot to obey an order that resulted in harm to human beings, including harm to the human giving the order. Sean had heard stories of robots experiencing total and permanent overload because of a conflict between the First and Second Laws; it was called brain-melt by some, because the robot's brain would actually overheat and melt crucial circuitry.

What Sean had seen at the death-scene rendered the theory of death-by-natural-causes unlikely. Even if the Sages were vulnerable to some hitherto unknown disease, Sean did not know of any disease process that could cause the kind of damage he had seen. Could the nanites have malfunctioned? Or, could some of the nanites within Sage Newton misidentified other nanites within him as foreign and essentially declared war? If that were the case, why would it not have happened before now? He would have to check on that idea. It was an area where his knowledge was too thin.

If it had not been murder or disease that did in Sage Newton, then that left suicide. But how? Sean felt that Sage Goodall knew the answer to at least some of his questions. Talking to the other Sages would be of no more use than was the audience granted them by Sage Reimann. What could the others know that their appointed spokesman had not already told him? That left him with the problem of how to get to Sage Goodall when Sage Goodall was not talking to anyone. Direct contact was out of the question, and audio or holographic communication would likely be rejected, although he would have to try it as a matter of course. The Caretakers would have to have some way of contacting the Sages in case of an emergency, and this would be especially true for Sage Goodall. Brian had identified him as the "nominal sovereign of Mercury" which meant that he ran things as much as they needed to be run, and that meant that he had to be accessible somehow.

At least he now knew the next three or four things he had to do. First, he would ask Sage Reimann if the robots serving Sage Newton had been checked for errors after his death, and specifically for Three-Law failures. Second, he would attempt to reach Sage Goodall by holographic port. If this failed, he would move to step three, which was to ask the Goodwright's to use their emergency channel to reach Sage Goodall. The fourth step was one he did not wish to consider, and he tried to put it out of his mind.

Sean enjoyed the low-gravity fall from the tree and returned to his cabin. He immediately went to the computer terminal and said, "Brian, is Sage Reimann available for a very brief conference?"

"I shall ask him, Sean."

A minute passed, and then Sean was startled by a voice coming from behind him saying, "You wanted me, Mr. Aldred?"

Sean turned and saw the image of

Sage Reimann standing in the middle of his cabin. "Yes, Sage Reimann, I have one question. Were Sage Newton's robotic servants all checked for Three-Law failures following the Sage's death?"

Sage Reimann nodded. "They were all checked thoroughly, and there was no evidence of Three-Law failures or of tampering. At the time of the Sage's death, all of his robotic servants were busy with high-concentration, time-consuming tasks, mainly consisting of maintenance on various life-support systems. This seems to be a coincidence, although it would be valuable knowledge to an outside agent who wanted to kill Sage Newton."

"Do you believe that it was an outside agent who killed the Sage?"

Reimann smiled. "I think it would take an extremely clever and resourceful and wealthy individual to leave Earth, come here, sneak in, kill a Sage without being infested, and escape without leaving a trail. I believe you Specialists call that a 'low-probability theory'."

Sean smiled. "Thank you for your time, Sage Reimann."

"Have you interviewed the other Sages yet?"

"No." Sean thought it would be better to keep his decision to not interview the other Sages to himself.

Sage Reimann spread his hands before him with the palms up and said, "Remember, we are at your disposal." His image shimmered and faded out.

Sean turned back to the computer terminal. "Brian, please attempt communication with Sage Goodall."

"I will try, Sean, but he continues to ignore attempts at communication, including the efforts already made by your colleagues."

Two minutes of silence passed before Brian said, "He continues to ignore us. All telemetry indicates that he is in good health and is awake."

"Can you put an holographic image into his cell without his permission?"

"No, Sean, the system is set up by the

Sages to prevent that."

"What about an audio-only message."

"Yes, that can be done. I should inform you that the Caretakers, Sage Reimann, Sage Marconi, Sage Faraday, and Sage Lavoisier have already done this. They received no response."

"I would like to try anyway. Let me know when the link is established."

"The link is established, Sean. Your next words will be transmitted directly into all rooms of Sage Goodall's cell, and at one hundred twenty percent of normal speaking volume. Give me a hand signal when you are done."

"Sage Goodall, this is Sean Aldred, one of the Specialists brought here by your fellow Sages to solve the mystery of Sage Newton's death. I know that you have refused communication with your fellow Sages, with the Caretakers, and with my colleagues, but I believe that you should make an exception on my behalf. The reasons that I think you should so is that I WILL be communicating with you soon, one way or the other. I would prefer to do this the easy way, but I will do it the hard way if need be. I think you would prefer it be the easy way as well, although I know that it is also possible that much of what the Sages are doing with the Specialists is some form of testing, and perhaps you do want me to do this the hard way. The choice is yours." Sean made a hand signal in the direction of the visual monitor on the computer terminal.

"Message completed. I will open the audio channel to Sage Goodall's cell in case he wants to respond, Sean."

"Thank you, Brian."

Sean sat and listened to the sound coming from Sage Goodall's cell for ten minutes. This consisted of a fire crackling, a chair sliding across the floor, papers shuffling, water running briefly, and a pencil being dropped on the floor. "Thank you for the attempt, Brian. Please tell me where I can find David or Melissa Goodwright."

"The Goodwright's are having lunch at the picnic table in the garden in front of the Caretakers' Cottage."

"Thank you, Brian. That will be all for now."

Sean looked in the pantry and the refrigerator in his kitchen nook, and put together a ham-and-cheese sandwich and a glass of cold spiced milk for his lunch. He put it on a tray and headed for the Caretakers' Cottage.

When he arrived at the Cottage, the Goodwright's were eating lunch at a picnic table surrounded by the fabulous flower garden. They waved to him to join them, and he sat beside Mr. Goodwright. "I brought my lunch and was hoping to catch you here."

Melissa Goodwright smiled and said, "You're welcome to join us, but I bet that you have more than lunch companions in mind."

Sean nodded, as he had decided on the direct approach. "I was wondering what you would do if you had to reach Sage Goodall. Is there an emergency communication system? After all, Sage Goodall is the sovereign of this planet, is he not?"

David Goodwright shook his head. "I'm sure that you already know that audio messages can be sent into a Sage's cell without his or her permission, but there is no way to make a Sage respond if he or she does not want to do so. We have tried talking to Sage Goodall many times, and will continue to do so, but he is not responding to us either. And, most operations on this planet run themselves. The sovereign's duties mostly involve approving, disapproving, or editing research projects by the other Sages."

"What if a fire broke out near a Sage's cell, in an access corridor?"

"The robot servants of that Sage would simultaneously work to extinguish the fire and safeguard the Sage."

"What if you believed that a Sage was having a medical emergency undetected by his robotic servants?"

Melissa Goodwright had lost her smile and was beginning to sound annoyed. "What could we do for a Sage that a Sage could not do for himself or herself?"

The thought flashed through Sean's mind that he could stage some kind of minor disaster to get Sage Goodall's attention, and then try to force a conversation. Then, in an instant, he had grasped at least part of what had been hovering at the fringe of his consciousness since the night before, and he also knew what he had to do next. After lunch, that is.

Sean smiled and said, "Did the seeds for your flowers come from Earth, or were they genetically engineered by the Sages?" The Goodwright's welcomed the sudden change in topic, and they discussed floriculture for thirty or forty minutes before Sean returned to his cabin.

When he got back, he sat down in front of the computer terminal and said, "Brian, please re-establish the audio-link to Sage Goodall's cell."

"Audio-link is re-established, Sean. Sage Goodall is eating lunch."

"Sage Goodall, I apologize for interrupting your lunch, but I wanted you to know that I have figured out that Sage

Newton committed suicide in a direct effort to lure Specialists to Mercury for some other purpose. I also know that Sage Newton acted against your wishes in this matter. I would like to discuss the real reason I'm here."

Sean was startled when a voice behind him said, "I was betting on you right from the beginning."

Sean swiveled and saw Sage Goodall's holographic image sitting in the middle of his cabin. The Sage was average in height and had snow-white hair and nearly-invisible eyebrows. His face was slim and he looked little older than a boy. Sean spread his hands before him and said, "So, why am I here?"

"To try to solve the mystery of the death of Sage Newton. But, you are right that that is not the final goal, but more of a lure and a test."

"A test?"

Sage Goodall smiled sadly and nodded. Sean slumped to the floor and was unconscious. He could not have smelled the anesthesia, as it was odorless. Sage Goodall quietly said, "Congratulations - you passed." He covered his face with his long, thin hands, which were trembling, and his holographic image shimmered out of existence. The robots were already there to collect Sean Aldred, which they did very gently.

Chapter Ten
The Pits of Midas

When Sean awoke, he was laying on a bed in a bedroom that was identical to the one he had left behind when he had gone to the Academy. At first he thought he was dreaming, but then he remembered his conversation with Sage Goodall. He sat up in bed, and saw the holographic image of Sage Goodall watching him from across the room. "Where am I?"

"You are still on Mercury, but now you occupy Cell Number Twenty-Two."

"Cell?"

"Yes, welcome to the Pits of Midas."

"Pits of Midas?"

"Sage Newton used to call this complex the 'Pits of Midas'. Are you familiar with the legend of King Midas?"

Sean's head was still fuzzy, but he vaguely remembered the legend. He nodded. "King Midas valued wealth so much that he wished that everything he touched turned to gold. His wish was granted, and then he couldn't eat or touch anyone. I think he turned his wife or his daughter to gold by accidentally touching them."

Sage Goodall nodded. "Right. And we cannot come into contact with people either. At least we have the holographic ports, though. And, the benefits are much greater than gold."

"What do you mean by 'we'?"

"You haven't figured it out yet? You have now joined our ranks, my boy." The Sage sounded oddly sad.

Things began to click for Sean. "We were lured here to solve the mystery of Sage Newton's death so that you could make us into Sages? The Sage's death was just a pretext?"

"Pretext! It was much more than that! You were right that I disagreed with Sage Newton's plan, but he sacrificed himself in order to bring new blood into the fold. However much I might have disagreed with Sage Newton's methods, and however much you might resent the position you are now in, we must both respect the price that Sage Newton paid to bring you here."

Sean shook his head. "Why not just ask for volunteers and screen them for acceptability?"

Sage Goodall nodded. "That was my plan, but Sage Newton objected on several grounds, which I am forced to admit were quite valid. A call for volunteers would likely have resulted in thousands of applications, and the screening process would have been unwieldy. Also, the people of Earth see us almost as gods, and a call for volunteers to join us would have damaged that image greatly. It would also have undermined our credibility as superior beings. That might sound pretentious or vain, but we are superior. That superiority is not racial or inherent, but due to longevity and the learning that comes with it, along with a tremendous amount of hard work; it is earned.

Sage Newton believed that ideal candidates already existed: the Specialists. You are all genetically engineered to be physically and cognitively superior, you have few family ties back on Earth because of your isolative training regimen, and you are well-trained in your own special form of research. Crime investigation is nothing more nor nothing less than a specialized form of scientific research. You will adapt well. You will be a new type of Sage, but not far from the Academics, qualitatively."

"Why didn't you secretly recruit volunteers from the ranks of Specialists, instead of engaging in this elaborate plot to get us here?"

"Would we have gotten the best of your kind? How long would it have remained secret? I understand your frustration and possible resentment and, as I said before, I never really supported this plan. However, I do have to express satisfaction with the results. We now have two new Sages who will add fresh ideas to our research and rejuvenate our social life, which had become quite stagnant, I assure you."

"Two new Sages? Why not four? Which other Specialist was chosen? What happened to the other two?"

Sage Goodall held up his hand to stop Sean. "Slow down, son. If you have gained anything, you have gained time. You and Specialist Cavanaugh were chosen because of your observed talents and for demographic reasons. Actually, she was a shoe-in right from the start because we needed a female. Between the two of you, you identified which of the many questions were the critical ones, and then found the answers to those questions. She, however, would have been chosen anyway, as she was only a half-step behind you in solving the mystery. The other two did not quite meet our standards."

Sean shook his head. "Michael Klein was one of the most renown Specialists on Earth. Why was he excluded?"

"Reputation does not always equate with quality. To be sure, he is a competent Specialist, but he lives off his reputation as much as off of his skill. And, to be frank, he has gotten lazy. He might have been reinvigorated by the transformation to Sage status, but that is not guaranteed. The testing here did not demonstrate he was likely to change. Mr. Lefevre was a close third to you and Ms. Cavanaugh."

"What will happen to them now?"

"They were told that you and Ms. Cavanaugh did not believe our warnings about contact with the Sages and died in an attempt at direct contact with me. It was not planned that way, but my silence provided us with a good cover-story for your disappearances."

"They will eventually find out otherwise, when Earth, in general, finds out there are two new Sages. How will you handle that?"

"We are working on a cover story, but you two will not be introduced to Earth for a while. That will give you time to adapt, before you have to deal with Earth's response to your new status."

"You said, before, that just choosing someone would tarnish your god-like images. How will you explain that with Celeste and me?"

Sage Goodall smiled faintly. "That one we already have figured out. While you were here, you were exposed to clean nanites, and we were left with no choice but to take you in. We still have to work on reconciling that story with the other story, but we will. One thing we always know: we have time."

"Clean nanites?"

"Yes, those are nanites not yet tagged to or identified with any person's DNA, leaving them open to bond with anyone."

Sean walked over to a mirror. He did not look any different.

"You were young to start with, so the transformation will not be very dramatic. I wonder whether your wrist still bothers you, or has that already been taken care of?"

Sean looked at his wrist; he wouldn't know if the ache was gone until he stressed it. He turned his back on Sage Goodall and pushed down his pants down far enough to see that his appendectomy scar was gone.

"That was going to be my next question. Is it gone?"

Sean straightened his clothes and turned back to the Sage. "Yes, it's gone. What will you do if we decide to not cooperate with you?"

Sage Goodall shrugged. "The question is more aptly put: What will YOU do if you decide to not cooperate with us? You cannot escape and, even if you did manage to do so, you are now fatal to any other living thing in the universe. If you need proof, the robots assigned to you can bring you any animal you choose - rat, mouse, cat, dog. Insects seem to be immune to us, which is probably due to their vastly different metabolic systems. A few of us even raise them as pets. What you do with your time for the rest of your life, which could be a very long time, is up to you."

Sean remembered something the Sage had said before. "Why did you need a female?"

"For our gene pool. We have surreptitiously taken sperm and egg samples from every Caretaker sent to us, and we did the same with all four of the Specialists. We hope that, in the future, we will be able to breed new members for our society instead of having to kidnap them."

A note of anger had crept into the Sage's voice with the last sentence. He signed and continued, "We also needed at least one more female to help our little group be more homogeneous. For whatever it is worth, I wholeheartedly apologize for what we have done. I hope that, in time, you will accept your situation and become a contributing member of our society. By the way, we can send some of your sperm sample Earth-side if you want to donate it there."

"How did Sage Newton kill himself?"

Sage Goodall sighed. "He was running two supposedly unrelated separate experiments. In one, he created a batch of clean nanites. In the other experiment, he obtained hair follicles from David Goodwright, supposedly to test cloning procedures. He exposed the nanites to the DNA in the hair samples, which caused the nanites to bond to that DNA. He then exposed himself to the nanites, which went to war with his nanites and destroyed him in a most painful and ugly fashion, as you know. As I said before, the price he paid was very high indeed. At least his death was rapid."

The Sage's image suddenly shimmered away, and Sean was alone. A noise from behind him startled him and he turned. A tall, dark blue robot had entered the room. "I am here to serve you, Sage Aldred." The voice was eerily familiar, and Sean placed it after a minute.

"Hello, Brian. So you were a robot all along?"

"Yes, Sean."

"And you knew what might be coming my way the whole time?"

"Yes, Sean. If you are angry with me, feel free to destroy me. I can be replaced."

Sean shook his head. "You and your Sage-masters seem to know me very well. You know that I will not vent my anger on you, especially when you carry my brother's name."

"We could not know that for a certainty, but we did know that the probability was low that you would accept my offer."

"Can I speak with Celeste?"

"Sage Goodall is waiting for Sage Cavanaugh to awaken, and then he will debrief her as he did you. After that, you will be welcome to speak with her. We anticipated that you two would want to talk this over, and have set time aside for it. In the meantime, can I get you anything, Sage Aldred?"

"You can go back to calling me 'Sean' for one thing. Beyond that, I haven't the foggiest idea what to do next."

"The other Sages want to throw you a welcome aboard and naming party. They did not know of the way you joined us, and they were not informed of your joining, until yesterday."

"A welcome aboard and naming party? What did you mean about the naming part?"

"Ah, you might have noticed that all the Sages carry the last names of famous thinkers. They developed a tradition of selecting new last names, to honor such great people, and to signify, to themselves and to others, that they are now new people. You might want to think about who you want to honor."

Sean looked in the mirror again, then smiled. I will be Sage Frankl, after Viktor Frankl, the psychiatrist who survived a Nazi concentration camp, to develop a theory of psychology and a philosophy I have found useful. It is a great approach to surviving enduring trauma."

"By the way, how long was I unconscious?"

"You were kept unconscious for three

days, as some of the transformation process can be painful, and we wanted to spare you that."

Sean sat down on the edge of the bed and said sarcastically, "How thoughtful."

He looked at the robot and realized that the hunk of metal in front of him was likely to be his best friend for a while. He knew that this was probably part of the plan, but he also knew that he would adapt. The Sages knew him well; they knew his adaptability quotient was extremely high.

"Brian, I would like you to begin compiling a list of ten crimes on Earth which occurred during the past ten years and are unsolved and are considered unsolveable. I might as well start with research that is familiar to me."

"As you wish, Sean." The robot's voice almost sounded happy.

Author Biography

Chris McCallister is a lifelong resident of Michigan, who is a clinical psychologist. He works for a non-profit agency that provides mental health services for low-income children, adolescents, and their families. At age fifteen, Chris had a diving injury causing quadriplegia.

Life in the Pits of Midas is his second book, following the novel, Coming Full Circle: Munising to Munising.

The other works of the author are:

    From the Ashes -- A novel about a group of idealists who try to change things in a struggling city, with possibly some supernatural help.
    The One True Legend of Lucather and Other Odd Tales -- This is a collection of short stories (urban fantasy and science fiction), plus a long poem).
    The Walks of the Others -- A novel aimed at the Young Adult audience, this is

science-fiction about a human colony trying to establish interaction with another sentient species on the planet they share.

Ode to Malgor, The Wholly Unbecoming, Who Unwittingly and Unintentionally aught Me an Aspect of Compassion -- This is a six-page writing exercise that I compose while hospitalized with pneumonia.

The works in progress at the time of this publication are:

Malgor the Magnificent -- This is a novel that I just started. It is planned to be a description of a man dealing with mental illness.

The Rings in My Life -- I just started this novel. It will follow four people across their lives as they figure out how to deal with unusual abilities.

Heisenberg Grenade – This novel is about a soldier who experiences a situation where he most certainly should have died but he instead survived unscathed. After being missing for a month, he suddenly shows up and has to explain himself. I have just started this one.

None of these works are related.

Made in the USA
Coppell, TX
08 March 2021

51471107R00062